The Painter

A Richard Jackson Book

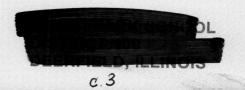

My daddy's a painter.
He paints pictures in his studio.

The Painter

by Peter Catalanotto

Orchard Books   New York

Every morning we make breakfast.
We're very good cooks.

We love to read the comics
and laugh so hard
we fall off our chair.

"Silly," says Mommy.
"Funny," says me.

I ask Daddy if we can go feed the ducks.
"Not today," says Daddy.

Play hopscotch?
"Not now," says Daddy.

Do a puzzle?
"Not yet," says Daddy.

Then he goes up to work in his studio.

Where I'm not allowed.

"It's too dangerous," Daddy says.

"You might get hurt."

At lunch I ask Daddy what is he painting.
"A car," says Daddy. "A blue one."

Yesterday he painted a butterfly.
Once it was a Dalmatian.

We love to dance after lunch.
We're very good dancers.

"Silly," says Mommy.
"Funny," says me.

I ask Daddy if we can kick my ball
over the house again.
"Not today," says Daddy.

Fly our kite?
"Not now," says Daddy.

Make a tent?

"Not yet," says Daddy.

Then he goes back to work in his studio.

At night it's my job to yell "Suppertime!"

After supper Daddy hangs a spoon on his nose
and turns lemons into apples.

I do magic too.
I tell Daddy I've lost my hand.
He looks everywhere for it.

"I give up," says Daddy.

"*Tah-dah!*" says me.

We're very good magicians.

I ask Daddy if we can do
a puppet show.
"Not now," says Daddy.

Read a book?
"Not yet," says Daddy.

Paint a picture?

"Not here," says Daddy.

"Here."

Mommy loves my pictures.
She says, "It looks like you'll be a painter
when you grow up."
I say, "I'm a painter *now*."

To Chelsea, always

Special thanks to Denys

Orchard Books, 95 Madison Avenue, New York, NY 10016

Manufactured in the United States of America. Printed by Barton Press, Inc. Bound by Horowitz/Rae.
Book design by Jean Krulis. The text of this book is set in 20 point ITC Zapf International Medium.
The illustrations are watercolor paintings reproduced in full color.

1 3 5 7 9 10 8 6 4 2

Library of Congress Cataloging-in-Publication Data
Catalanotto, Peter.   The painter / Peter Catalanotto.   p.   cm.   "A Richard Jackson book"—Half t.p.
Summary: Although her father is busy working as an artist at home, he still finds time to spend with his daughter.
ISBN 0-531-09465-0.—ISBN 0-531-08765-4 (lib. bdg.)
[1. Artists—Fiction.   2. Fathers and daughters—Fiction.]   I. Title.
PZ7.C26878Pai   1995   [E]—dc20   94-48808